Printed in the U.S.A.

ISBN 0-7172-8290-2

JIM HENSON'S MUPPETS

IN

Piggy Isn't Talking

A Book About Communication

By Andrew Gutelle • Illustrated by Tom Leigh

GROLIER

There is nothing better than having a good friend. And as far as Piggy was concerned, she had one of the best.

Kermit had been Piggy's friend for a long, long time. They walked to school together. They played on the same soccer team. They had long, happy conversations on the telephone.

Of course, Kermit was also Fozzie Bear's friend. They rode bikes together. They sat side by side in Mr. Bumper's class. When Fozzie heard a new joke, he always told it to Kermit first.

But that was okay with Piggy. Somehow, Kermit always found enough time to be with both of them.

On the last day of school, Kermit, Piggy, and Fozzie ate lunch together in the cafeteria.

"I can't believe we'll be going to day camp together!" said Fozzie, biting into his avocado-and-honey sandwich. "My dad says Camp Wockawocka's the best!"

"I hope we get to play soccer," said Kermit as he carefully broke his graham cracker in half and handed one piece to Piggy.

Piggy gave Kermit several sections of an orange she had just peeled. "Don't be silly, Kermit! Of course we will."

On the first day of camp, Piggy waited outside her house. Before long, the camp bus stopped in front of her.

The bus was packed with campers. Kermit and Fozzie were sitting together. Piggy wanted to sit with them, but she was the last kid on the bus route. The only empty seat was way at the back, next to Janice.

Kermit waved as Piggy walked past him. Piggy waved back and then sat down.

Janice told Piggy about her new bathing suit. As Piggy listened, she heard a familiar laugh near the front of the bus. *Fozzie must have told Kermit a new joke,* she thought. *Maybe Kermit will tell it to me when we get to camp.*

When the bus arrived, everyone hurried off. Piggy ran to join Kermit and Fozzie. She was about to ask Kermit to tell her Fozzie's joke when someone tapped her on the shoulder. She turned and saw a Camp Wockawocka counselor.

"Excuse me, but I think you're in the wrong place," he said.

"I'm the counselor of this group," he explained. "We're called the Grasshoppers."

"Can't I be a Grasshopper?" asked Piggy.

"I'm sorry, but this is a boys' group," the counselor said. "Let's see where you belong."

The counselor checked the list on his clipboard. "Well, Piggy, it seems you're going to be a Ladybug," he told her. Then he sent her to join Skeeter, Janice, and the other Ladybugs.

At Camp Wockawocka, Ladybugs are always busy. Piggy should have been able to forget about Kermit. But as the Ladybugs walked to the swimming pool, she saw Kermit and the Grasshoppers playing soccer. When the Ladybugs went on their nature hike, she saw the Grasshoppers inside the arts-and-crafts tent.

Kermit looks like he's having fun, thought Piggy. *He doesn't even seem to miss me at all.*

Everyone at camp ate lunch together. Piggy hoped to sit with Kermit, but his picnic table was full of Grasshoppers.

Piggy sat with Janice and Skeeter. She watched as Kermit broke his graham cracker in half and handed a piece to Fozzie. *He used to share his graham crackers with me,* she thought, sighing loudly.

"Piggy, is something wrong?" asked Skeeter.

Piggy was embarrassed that she missed Kermit so much, so she didn't say a word.

All afternoon, Piggy could see how much fun Kermit was having without her. *Maybe Kermit and I aren't friends anymore,* she thought. *Maybe he just wants to be friends with Fozzie and the other boys.*

At the end of the day, the Ladybugs were the last group to board the bus. Piggy walked glumly past Kermit and Fozzie.

"Isn't camp great, Piggy?" asked Kermit.

Piggy didn't think so, but somehow she couldn't tell Kermit. So she didn't say a word. She just smiled weakly and went to her seat.

The next morning, Piggy felt more hopeful. *Maybe today will be better,* she told herself.

But when Piggy boarded the camp bus, she sighed. All the kids had taken the same seats. There was her seat next to Janice.

It was the same every day that week. Piggy
wanted to tell Kermit that she missed playing
with him, but she hardly saw him. When they
did see each other for a few minutes, she was too
upset to talk about it. So she didn't say a word.

When the weekend came, Piggy was glad she wouldn't have to go to camp. On Saturday, Kermit stopped by her house. "Fozzie has a new kite," he told her. "Do you want to help us fly it?"

"I don't think so," Piggy replied. "I have a lot of things to do at home today."

"Piggy, is something wrong?" Kermit asked.

Piggy didn't say a word. She just shook her head no and closed the door.

That Sunday, Piggy went over to Mrs. Kodiak's house. Mrs. Kodiak was making some cookies, and Piggy had promised to help.

All afternoon, Piggy was very quiet. When the cookies were done, she didn't even want any.

"Is something wrong?" Mrs. Kodiak asked.

"Oh, not really," Piggy replied.

Mrs. Kodiak put her arm around Piggy. "Dear, you've hardly said a word all day. Something's bothering you. But I can't help you if you don't talk to me."

Piggy sighed. "It's my friend Kermit," she said finally.

Piggy told Mrs. Kodiak about what had been happening at camp. "I don't think Kermit wants to be my friend anymore," she said sadly.

"What does Kermit have to say about all this?" Mrs. Kodiak asked.

"I haven't talked to him," Piggy admitted.

"Piggy," said Mrs. Kodiak, "you have got to tell Kermit the things you just told me. Good friends need to talk to one another. That's what we call communication."

Piggy knew Mrs. Kodiak was right. So when she got home, she dialed Kermit's number.

"Hi, Piggy," said Kermit. "How are you?"

Piggy took a deep breath. "Not so good, Kermit. Camp isn't turning out to be much fun."

Piggy talked and talked. She told Kermit that she missed playing with him and couldn't understand why he didn't miss her, too.

"I *do* miss you. But I'm a Grasshopper, and you're a Ladybug!" said Kermit.

"That may be true," said Piggy. "But I'm a friend and you're a friend. And friends find ways to be together."

The next morning, when Piggy got on the camp bus, Fozzie was sitting next to Janice. The seat next to Kermit was empty.

"I saved you a seat," said Kermit.

Piggy sat down. "I'm sorry if I upset you," said Kermit. "I was so busy being a Grasshopper that I didn't think about how you might feel. I'm really glad you told me."

Even though she was still a Ladybug and Kermit was still a Grasshopper, Piggy was really glad she and Kermit were talking again.

During the morning sing-along, Kermit sat at the end of his group so Piggy could sit next to him. Kermit sat next to Piggy at lunch, too. By the end of the day, Piggy felt much better.

When Piggy boarded the bus to go home, she smiled at Kermit and walked past the empty seat next to him. Fozzie was sitting quietly at the back, next to Janice.

"Fozzie, why don't you sit next to Kermit?" said Piggy. "I sat with him a lot today and you didn't. Besides, I'd like to sit with Janice. She's my friend, too."

Fozzie and Piggy switched seats. And Piggy and Janice talked the whole way home.

Let's Talk About Communication

Piggy was very unhappy about the way Kermit was treating her at camp. Luckily, she was able to tell him about it. Kermit changed the way he was acting, and that made both of them feel a lot better. Talking and listening like that is what we call *communication.*

Here are some questions about communication for you to think about:

Have you ever had feelings about something that made you very mad or very sad? Did you tell someone? What happened?

Why do you think that it's important to tell people how you are feeling?